Demi's Reflective Fables

Retold and illustrated by Demi

Publishers • GROSSET & DUNLAP • New York

Copyright © 1988 by Demi. All rights reserved. Published by Grosset & Dunlap, Inc.,
a member of The Putnam Publishing Group, New York.
Published simultaneously in Canada. Printed in Singapore.
Library of Congress Catalog Card Number: 87-83261
ISBN 0–448–09281–6   A B C D E F G H I J

The Mirror

A certain dragoness had never seen a mirror before. She did not even know what a mirror was. One day her husband flew home with one and proudly presented it to her.

Picking up the mirror and looking into it, the dragon's wife was thunderstruck. "My husband has brought home another wife!" she cried to her mother.

Then the mother dragon peered into the mirror. "Not only that!" she loudly exclaimed. "He has brought her mother, too!"

Reflect on this: What you don't properly know, you won't properly see.

Note: Cover the story with the front jacket flap and use the "mirror" to reflect the art as you think about the meaning of each fable.

Two Pairs of Eyes

Two children were playing outdoors
when a butterfly suddenly flew overhead.
"How beautiful he is!" said one child.
"Oh no, he is ugly," said the other.
The children argued back and forth for a long time,
but they could not agree.
Finally one child said to the other, "I will get someone
else to look at the butterfly and he will tell you that I
am right."
But the butterfly's features were not changed by
anyone else's comments. The two children had
different views, not because they wished to argue,
but because each saw the butterfly through his
own eyes.

Beauty is in the eye of the beholder.

The Bat
and the Weasels

A bat fell on the ground and was pounced
upon by a weasel. He begged the weasel to spare
his life. But the weasel refused, saying that weasels
are by nature the enemy of all birds.

The bat assured the weasel that he was not a bird but
a mouse. Thus the bat managed to save his life.

Sometime later, the bat was caught again, this time by a
different weasel. Again he begged not to be eaten. But this
weasel said, "I'm going to eat you, for I love to eat mice."

At that the bat assured the weasel that he was not a
mouse but a bird. And thus, for the second time, the bat
saved his life.

Keep your wits about you always and turn
bad circumstances into good.

The Owl
and the Turtledove

A turtledove met an owl.

"Where are you off to?" asked the turtledove.

"I am moving to the East," replied the owl.

"Why are you moving?" asked the turtledove.

"The birds here don't like the sound of my hoot," the owl replied. "That's why I'm moving to the East."

A few days later, the turtledove met the owl again. This time the owl was flying north.

"It would be a good thing if you could change the way you hoot," said the turtledove. "Otherwise, wherever you move, there will be birds who won't like the way you sound."

You can move to the East or to the West;
you can move to the North or to the South;
but you can never move away from
yourself.

The Boar Who Declared War on the Forest

A certain boar thought his strength was magnificent and wanted all the animals in the forest to notice. He was mad when not many did, so he started rushing wildly about. But the boar was most unlucky.

The first tree he charged into cut a gash in his hide while the next knocked one of his tusks crooked. Under the circumstances, what could such a strong boar do but completely lose his temper?

The boar angrily declared that the whole forest was his enemy. He attacked the trees, charging them head on, hurling his weight at them, biting and kicking. His eyes flashed fire and the animals quaked at the sound of his bellow, as if a real war were being waged.

But the boar was unwilling to let it go at that. Although badly wounded, he felt he had to shatter at least one more tree.

With a bound he hurled himself into a tree, but this time his tusks stuck fast in the bark. Utterly defeated, he was unable to set himself free.

How humiliated he was when the monkeys had to pull him out by the tail.

It is best to deal with your frustration in a positive way.

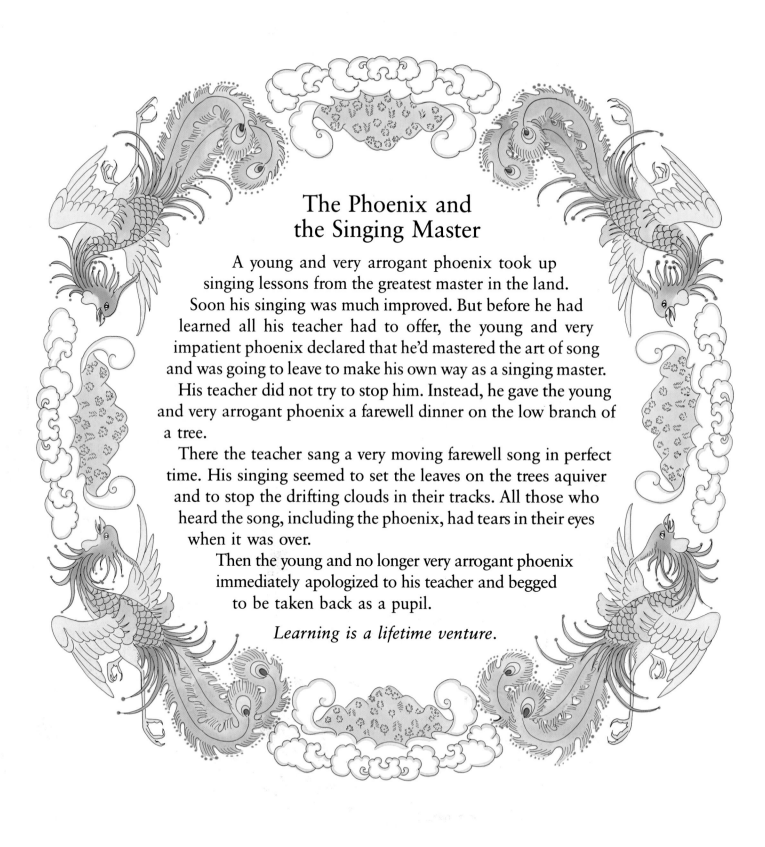

The Phoenix and the Singing Master

A young and very arrogant phoenix took up singing lessons from the greatest master in the land. Soon his singing was much improved. But before he had learned all his teacher had to offer, the young and very impatient phoenix declared that he'd mastered the art of song and was going to leave to make his own way as a singing master.

His teacher did not try to stop him. Instead, he gave the young and very arrogant phoenix a farewell dinner on the low branch of a tree.

There the teacher sang a very moving farewell song in perfect time. His singing seemed to set the leaves on the trees aquiver and to stop the drifting clouds in their tracks. All those who heard the song, including the phoenix, had tears in their eyes when it was over.

Then the young and no longer very arrogant phoenix immediately apologized to his teacher and begged to be taken back as a pupil.

Learning is a lifetime venture.

The Ugly Crab

Once there was a big, ugly crab with purple spots who did not realize that he was big and ugly with purple spots. One day he saw another crab who was drawing in the sand with a stick. The big, ugly crab immediately asked this artist to draw his picture. The artist was willing, and in no time at all a marvelous likeness appeared in the sand.

But the big, ugly crab felt that the artist had done him an injustice, and so made him do the picture all over. The artist tried again and again, adding rocks to emphasize the spots and sprinkling on darker sands for shading.

By this time a crowd of smaller crabs had gathered around, all admiring the likeness and the artist's ingenuity. But the big, ugly crab was still dissatisfied, claiming that the artist made him look big and ugly and spotted.

"I have beautified you as much as I possibly can!" the artist angrily exclaimed. "If I were to draw you exactly as you really appear, the picture would be hideous!"

And the other crabs all agreed.

*It is very hard to see yourself
objectively.*

The Bird Who Was Killed by Kindness

A beautiful wild bird alighted on the branch
of a tree that grew in the Emperor's garden.
The Emperor was enchanted by the bird and ordered
a golden cage for it to live in. He held feasts for the bird
in his great hall and commanded the most beautiful music
be played for it.
But in spite of all this luxury, the bird grew to look quite
wretched. Soon it seemed to be in a daze, not able to swallow
a morsel of food or to drink a single drop of wine.
After three days, the bird died.
At first the Emperor was bewildered, then he grew very
sad. He realized at last that he had killed his new friend
by kindness. He had entertained the wild bird as he
himself liked to be entertained, not as the bird
liked to be treated.

*Reflect on how you treat
your friends.*

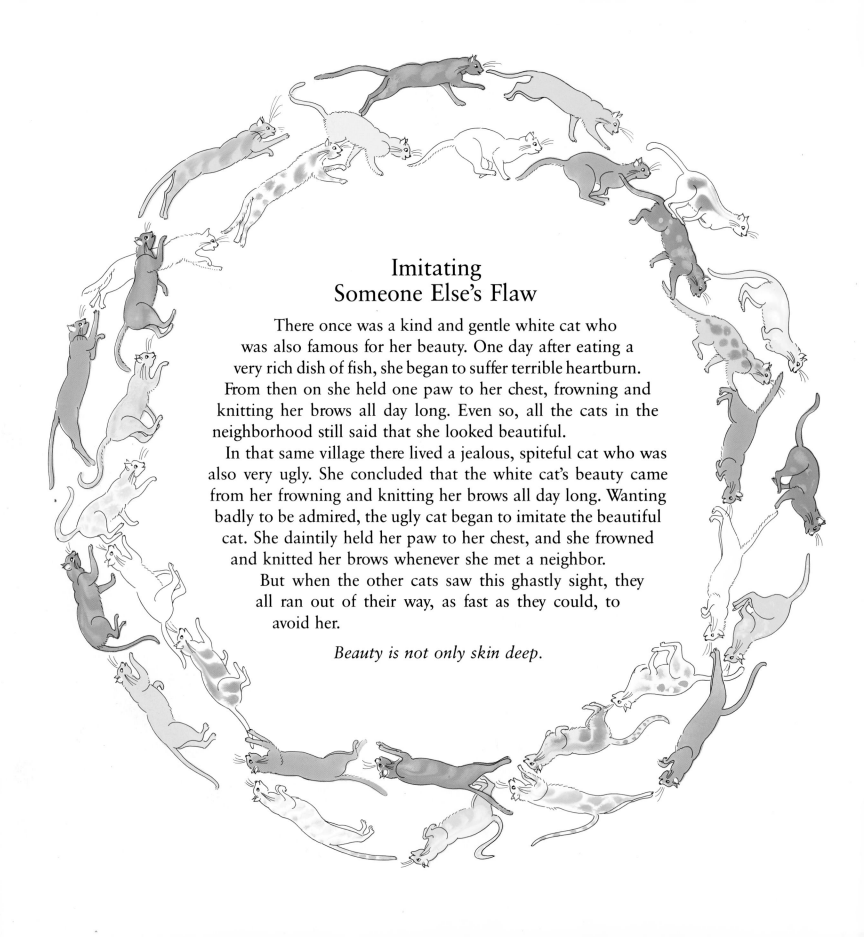

Imitating
Someone Else's Flaw

There once was a kind and gentle white cat who
was also famous for her beauty. One day after eating a
very rich dish of fish, she began to suffer terrible heartburn.
From then on she held one paw to her chest, frowning and
knitting her brows all day long. Even so, all the cats in the
neighborhood still said that she looked beautiful.

In that same village there lived a jealous, spiteful cat who was
also very ugly. She concluded that the white cat's beauty came
from her frowning and knitting her brows all day long. Wanting
badly to be admired, the ugly cat began to imitate the beautiful
cat. She daintily held her paw to her chest, and she frowned
and knitted her brows whenever she met a neighbor.

But when the other cats saw this ghastly sight, they
all ran out of their way, as fast as they could, to
avoid her.

Beauty is not only skin deep.

Two Peacocks

One morning a green peacock looked at himself in the mirror and asked his wife, "Who is handsomer—me or the white peacock who lives in the reeds?"

"You are definitely handsomer," his wife replied.

Now the white peacock was known far and wide for being a very handsome bird. So the green peacock, not satisfied, asked the question of the timid hummingbird. "How could he be compared to you?" was the hummingbird's reply.

Later the scavenger bird arrived as usual to peck over the green peacock's leftover lunch. The peacock asked the question once more. "You are by far more handsome!" the scavenger bird replied.

The next day the green peacock spied the brilliant white peacock glistening in the sun. He went home, looked in the mirror, and knew that he was not as handsome as the white peacock.

Lying awake that night he reflected: "My wife loves me, the hummingbird is afraid of me, and the scavenger bird wants something from me. No wonder they all say what they know I want to hear!"

Flattering words are not always true, and true words are not always flattering.

A Butterfly's Dream

Once upon a time a caterpillar fell asleep on a blade of grass that gently swayed back and forth in the breeze. He began to dream that he was a butterfly, floating like a petal in the wind.

Soon the other butterflies welcomed him. "Come with us," they called. So he flitted with them from flower to flower, quenching his thirst with dew from the rose and enjoying the perfume of the lily and the jasmine.

The butterflies seemed to live from minute to minute. Unlike the other creatures of the earth, they did not have a warlike nature, worries of life, fears of death, or complicated feelings like jealousy.

Too soon the caterpillar awoke and was astonished to find that he was still a caterpillar. Or was he? "Did I dream myself a butterfly?" he wondered. "If you compare a caterpillar and a butterfly, the difference between them is only in their material forms." Finally he said to himself, "Who knows? Perhaps my life is only a butterfly's dream."

This is truly a reflective fable.

The Rooster
and the Herons

A farmer once had a magnificent rooster.
If a weasel entered the farmyard, the rooster always put
up a courageous fight. At the sight of something good to
eat, the rooster always shared the food with the other fowl.
He faithfully watched over the farm each night and announced
the sunrise each morning, maintaining order on the farm. In spite
of these fine qualities, the rooster feared the farmer might choose
him for the dinner pot. Why? Simply because he was so near at hand.
One day two beautiful herons flew onto the farm. They devoured all
the fish in the farmer's pond and pecked their way into the grain and
beans. In spite of this the farmer neglected the other fowl and cherished
these wild birds. Why? Simply because they had come from far away.
The farm soon fell into disrepair. When the farmer realized
he had not seen his rooster for many days, he went to look for
him. But the rooster had fled, taking the hen and chicks away
with him. "Because I neglected what was most valuable,
I am filled with regret," the farmer cried. "Never can
I hope to regain what I have lost, especially
my magnificent rooster!"

Know what is most valuable
and treasure it.

The River God
and the Ocean God

Once upon a time in autumn there was a minor flood. The waters of many small rivers overflowed into a big river, enlarging it so greatly that the buffaloes on one bank could hardly see the horses on the other. As a result, the River God began to think that he was as great as great could be. His head swelled with pride as he followed the torrential flow of the river eastward.

Imagine his surprise when he finally came to the ocean and found it vast and boundless. There he saw towering waves so high that he could not help heaving a great sigh.

Said the River God to the Ocean God, "If I had not traveled here today and seen your size with my own eyes, I would have remained very stupid. I thought I was as great as great could be."

To this the Ocean God humbly replied, "There is no body of water on Earth as large as the ocean. Thousands of rivers incessantly flow into it, but the ocean never feels full. Even so, I am never proud and arrogant because I know I am only a product of nature. Compared to the greatness of Heaven and Earth, I am no more than the smallest stone on the side of the tallest mountain."

The more you know, the more you
realize how much there
is still to learn.

Author's Note

Reflective Fables began with my reflections on a
Chinese mirror. The bronze mirrors of ancient China
were not only used as looking glasses, but were also believed
to have magical powers. They could ward off evil influences,
ensure good fortune and numerous children for their owners, and
some were even used to forecast the future.

The mirrors were called "lucks" and were treasured accordingly. A
soldier going off to war would wear a mirror on his breast to protect him
from harm. A new bride going to her husband's home would hold one over
her heart so that no ill fortune would befall her. A young man setting out for
a new post would welcome a mirror as a gift to help him win a quick
promotion. Physicians used them to diagnose their patients' troubles. Mirrors
were placed over the hearts of the deceased to protect their souls in the
hereafter.

The smooth, polished front surfaces were used as reflectors. The back
surfaces were enriched with cast designs which symbolized the laws of the
heavens. Written inscriptions, reflective stories, and animal motifs were
incorporated into the designs, all as inspiration to the attainment of
Heaven.

Because the mirrors themselves are so beautiful, and the whole
idea of reflective surfaces so inviting, I have chosen to combine
them in this book so that all who read these ancient
fables will gain from their magic and their light. To
be as bright as the sun, to keep thoughts and
and sights high, to have reflective
thinking, all seemed
right.